HAWKE & CO

BOOK ONE

The New Neighbours

Catherine Cooper

First published in Great Britain in 2010 by
PENGRIDION BOOKS
39 St Chad's Close, Shropshire, TF1 3EP

www.pengridion.co.uk
pengridionbooks@btinternet.com

© Text Catherine Cooper 2010
© Illustrations Natalie Furnival 2010
© cover design Catherine Cooper 2010
The moral rights of the author, illustrator
and designer have been asserted.

A CIP catalogue record of this book
is available from the British Library.

ISBN 978-0-9563093-1-0

Typeset in Cochin 12pt
by Chandler Book Design,
www.chandlerbookdesign.co.uk

Printed in Great Britain by the
MPG Books Group, Bodmin and King's Lynn.

BOOK ONE

The New Neighbours

written by

Catherine Cooper

illustrated by

Natalie Furnival

cover designed by Catherine Cooper

Also available from Pengridion Books
by Catherine Cooper

The Golden Acorn
The Adventures of Jack Brenin
Book One

for

Iris, Mary, Bill and Sam

without whom this book would not have
been possible

CHAPTERS

HAWKE&CO

HAWKE

Valentine Sibelius Hawke

SPIKE

Stephen Pike

SEBASTIAN

Sebastian Amadeus Hawke

'The ballista, is a weapon of war, we are at war with the people next door and you are supposed to jump on this end and send that rock flying. Got it?'

1
The Ballista

'Fire!' yelled Hawke from behind the old beech tree at the bottom of the garden.

'Where?' Spike shouted.

Hawke could see Spike looking worried and getting ready to run.

'Can't see no flames Hawke, where's the fire?'

'There isn't one, I'm talking about the ballista.'

Spike looked puzzled and started to examine his hands.

'Haven't got no blisters.'

Hawke came out from behind the tree and pointed to the contraption on the grass, next to where his best friend Spike was standing.

'I've told you twice already, what we've made is called a ballista.'

They both looked at the weapon; it wasn't perfect but Hawke was sure it would work. They'd made it out of whatever they'd been able to find. Spike was supposed to jump onto the raised end and send a large piece of rock, which they'd borrowed from the rockery, flying through the air and over the fence.

'Tell me again why we're trying to get the rock into next-door's garden Hawke.'

'Because last week, when that snobby lot moved in, I was having a look through the hole in the fence and one of them comes and stares right back at me. Then he calls me an *oik* and stabs his finger at me through the hole. If I hadn't moved back quick he'd have poked my eye out. Next thing he's blocked the hole up.'

Spike looked towards the fence to where Hawke was pointing.

'There's a hole there now.'

'I know, I unblocked it when he'd gone. Not his fence to go messing with, but we're going to get them back… I'm not having nobody call me an *oik*.'

'But how do you know they're snobby Hawke?'

'Only snobs call people *oiks* and I heard their Dad telling them they could have a real den for the garden, whatever they wanted, a fort, tree house, it was up to them; you should have heard them bragging about how they'd have the best den in the street.'

'Better than ours?'

Hawke looked sadly at their den, it used to be the garden shed; his Dad had emptied it when the new garage had been built. His parents had said they could use it. The shed's only contents were a rickety chair and a multitude of insects and spiders. It was now called *The Den* but it was far from ideal. Hawke had to share it with his little brother Sebastian; he had to share everything with Sebastian. Hawke sighed.

'Much better than ours Spike.'

'They've already got a big pool and they're having a new den too?'

'Yep, told you they were snobs.'

Hawke wandered over to the fence and put his eye to the hole. He could just see the sides of the pool at the top of next-door's garden. For days now he'd listened to them splashing about and keeping cool; they'd not invited anyone to join them. Hawke chuckled; the rock they were about to launch was going to sail over the fence, land right in the middle of the pool and make a big hole. That should put an end

4

to their fun. They'd have a big surprise waiting for them when they got home. It was a good plan, a master plan, and he thought Spike had understood it. Hawke sighed and went back to join Spike and began explaining again.

'The ballista is a weapon of war; we are at war with the people next door and you are supposed to jump on this end and send that rock flying. Got it?'

Spike nodded slowly and looked thoughtful. Hawke continued.

'So when I shout *fire*, you jump.'

Spike nodded again.

'OK Hawke, I think I've got it this time.'

Sebastian appeared out of nowhere. He looked at the ballista before speaking to his brother.

'That looks dangerous, Mum and Dad won't be pleased if they see it.'

Hawke glowered at Sebastian and pushed him away from the ballista.

'No one asked for your opinion little brother.'

Sebastian ignored Hawke and had a closer look at the contraption.

'You know it's not going to work don't you?'

'Why not?' asked Spike.

Sebastian folded his arms and shook his blonde curls before giving Spike and Hawke his verdict.

'The angle of trajectory's wrong.'

Spike looked puzzled.

'What's a *trad ectory*?'

Hawke groaned; he knew Sebastian was about to launch into a long explanation and they didn't have any time to waste. Their new neighbours might arrive home any minute.

'Ignore him Spike, just concentrate on jumping onto this end of the plank and getting that rock over the fence into next-door's pool.'

'OK Hawke; so there isn't any fire?'

'Fire!' exclaimed Sebastian, 'you know you're

not allowed to play with fire.'

Hawke shook his head and sighed.

'There never was a fire, it's what I shout when I want him to jump.'

Spike frowned.

'Can't you just shout *jump* and then I'll know what to do?'

'Jump it is,' grumbled Hawke crossly as he stomped off to shelter again behind the trunk of the beech tree.

Sebastian didn't move. Hawke knew his brother would gloat if the ballista didn't work, he took a deep breath then yelled, 'Jump!'

Spike swung his arms and bent his knees but before his feet left the ground Sebastian interrupted him.

'You ought to jump off something higher; you'll get a lot more power that way. Even then it's not exactly how a ballista works, you know, this is more like a see-saw and I really don't think…'

'Now what?' shouted Hawke as he came out from behind the tree and glowered at Spike, 'why didn't you jump? I thought we'd agreed I'd shout jump and not fire.'

'Sebastian says I need to jump off something, I'll go and get the chair out of the den.'

Without waiting for a reply, Spike went off to the shed and came back with the only chair they possessed and positioned it so he could easily jump onto the plank.

'Ready,' Spike called and began swinging his arms.

Hawke went back behind the tree, 'Jump!' he yelled, then crossed his fingers, hoping his carefully thought out plan was going to work. He peeped round the tree trunk and watched Spike land perfectly on the end of the plank. The rock went flying into the air then Sebastian began counting.

'Three… two… one… and smash!'

There was a self-satisfied look on Sebastian's face as the rock crashed straight through the window of the den followed by a resounding thud as it hit the inside wall. The shed wobbled, and then, as if in slow motion began to collapse like a house of cards.

'Nooooo!' wailed Hawke.

Spike looked embarrassed and swallowed hard, 'Ooops, sorry.'

'I told you the trajectory was wrong,' Sebastian said smugly.

By now the whole shed was flat on the grass, the smashed window hidden underneath the debris of what had once been their den.

'Maybe we should have sorted that *trajectory* out Hawke.'

'Maybe you should have jumped better.'

As usual whenever there was a problem, Sebastian disappeared. Hawke looked around expecting to see his Mum. He held his breath but she didn't appear at the kitchen door; she obviously hadn't heard the crash. Hawke began thinking fast to try and avoid getting into trouble.

'Jump on the ballista,' he ordered Spike.

'I just did Hawke!'

'Again stupid, break it up, if we put the pieces with the shed no one will ever know it was us!'

They quickly wrecked what was left of their weapon of war. It wasn't too difficult; Spike's jump had almost broken it in two.

Hawke sat on the chair to think. This was his sign he wasn't to be disturbed. He knew Spike wouldn't interrupt him; thinking was something Spike wasn't very good at. He was angry, his plan had failed and his dream of making their den the envy of the neighbourhood was now in ruins, or more accurately, splinters. He knew it was beyond repair, a lot of the wood looked rotten. He had to work something out quick or else he'd be in big trouble, but he was finding it hard to concentrate.

Hawke sat on the chair to think.

Just as he was beginning to despair an idea popped into his head. The cross expression on his face turned into a rather large grin. He was about to explain his new master plan to Spike when his Mum appeared at the kitchen door. She took her headphones off and called down the garden.

'Valentine, Sebastian, dinner's ready.'

Hawke cringed. He hated his stupid name, just his luck to have been born on Valentine's Day. His middle name wasn't any better either, Sibelius, after his Dad's favourite composer. Another shudder ran down Hawke's spine as his Mum called him again. Spike nudged him.

'Your mum's calling you.'

'I know,' Hawke snapped, 'I just hate that name.'

'It could have been worse!' Sebastian shouted as he ran past them towards the kitchen.

'What could possible be worse?' Hawke grumbled.

'Romeo!' Sebastian yelled before he disappeared into the kitchen.

Hawke scowled at Spike so he'd know not to laugh.

'Better be off for my dinner too, see you tomorrow.'

Spike looked back at the pile of wood on the grass.

'Where're we going to meet now the den's flat?'

'By the tree, hopefully not for too long, I'm working on something.'

'What about them next door?'

'We've got all summer to sort them out, we need a new den first.'

Spike nodded slowly, took a last look at the remains of the old den, then shoved his hands in his pockets before making his way to the gate.

Once Spike was out of sight, Hawke dropped to his knees. He waited until he was sure he was alone and then began to cry loudly. It wasn't long before his mum came running out of the kitchen.

'What's the matter Valentine?'

Hawke sobbed even louder and made his body shake.

'Oh!' gasped his Mum when she saw the shed then gave a shrill shriek as she dashed down the garden.

'Valentine, are you hurt? What happened?'

'*So far so good*,' thought Hawke but he didn't stop shaking or crying as his Mum checked to see if he was alright.

'If… I'd… had… a… proper… den… it… wouldn't… have… happened…'

Hawke was glad Spike had gone; he wouldn't have wanted him to see his Mum with her arms around him. Now he knew he wasn't going to be in trouble it was time for part two of his plan.

'Se... bas... tian... could... have... been... hurt... if... he'd... been... in... side...'

'I knew you shouldn't have been playing in that rotten old shed, I told your Dad it wasn't safe, it's a good job neither of you were inside, now dry your eyes and come in for dinner, I'll have a word with your Dad and we'll see what we can do.'

Hawke gave his Mum a wobbly smile and blew his nose on the tissue she'd given him. He hung his head as he walked slowly back to the house, he didn't want her to see how pleased he looked. It wouldn't be long before he'd have a brand new den. His Mum and Dad wouldn't risk anything happening to his brother. Sebastian was clever; he could read music, play the piano and was also having violin lessons. Not only could he sing like an angel, but with a head full of blond curls and big blue eyes, he actually looked like one too. Hawke was the complete opposite; he had no musical talent, couldn't sing and his short dark hair was always a mess.

By the time they reached the kitchen, Hawke was sure his Mum and Dad would get him a real den. It would be better than anything the snobs next door would have. Maybe his ballista plan hadn't been such a bad one after all.

2

The New Name

For the rest of that week Hawke and Spike met by the old beech tree at the bottom of the garden. After the remains of the old shed had been taken to the tip they'd set up a couple of goals and kicked Spike's football around, but it was too hot to run about for long. They'd spent a lot of time sitting in the shade under the tree listening to the two kids next door, keeping cool and having fun, in their undamaged pool.

Hawke hadn't been in a very good mood since their den had collapsed, but today was different; he'd got some great news to tell Spike.

'It's tomorrow!' Hawke said as soon as Spike arrived.

'It's not, it's today.'

'I know it's today, it's tomorrow we get our new den, it's arriving in the morning.'

'Aw great!'

'It's on stilts and it's got a ladder, windows and a real door that locks too. Dad got it in a sale, he says there might be a few things we need to do to it, but by lunchtime tomorrow, our new den will rise from the ashes like the phoenix.'

Spike frowned.

'So there was a fire?'

'There wasn't, it's just a saying.'

'Don't they have a saying for splinters?'

Hawke ignored Spike and continued with his news.

'I've been watching next door through the hole in the fence, they haven't got their den yet so we'll be first to have a new one.'

'What they like next door?'

'Don't know, not got a good look at them. You can't see much through the hole and there's a jungle at the bottom of their garden. Mum says they're twins; I know they're called Tom and Sam, I've heard their Dad calling them.'

'How old are they?'

'Don't know but Mum said they're going to be at our school next term, they might even be in our class.'

'That'll be good.'

'No it won't, we don't like them, remember?'

'We've not seen them yet so how'd you know we don't like them?'

'I just do, right.'

Spike frowned.

Hawke decided to change the subject.

you can't see much through the hole

'By tomorrow we need to have a name, something to call ourselves so we can put it on a sign over the door of the new den, then those boys next door will know who they're dealing with.'

'What kind of a name Hawke?'

'A really good one.'

Hawke sat on the chair and took up his thinking position. He watched Spike wander over to the fence and look through the hole.

'Oh by the way, I forgot to tell you, Dad said to mind the fence, he only painted it an hour ago.'

It was too late. When Spike turned round he had a green ring around his eye and a smudge on the side of his nose. Hawke couldn't stop laughing; he was almost doubled up when Sebastian arrived.

'You shouldn't laugh at other people's misfortunes.'

When Spike turned round he had a green ring
around his eye and a smudge on the side of his nose.

'He looks so funny,' spluttered Hawke.

Sebastian went over to Spike and had a good look at his face.

'That needs sorting out before it dries.'

As Spike searched his pockets for a tissue, Sebastian gave his brother a scornful look then took charge.

'Come with me Spike, Mum will get rid of it for you.'

Hawke watched them until they disappeared through the kitchen door then settled down again to think.

It wasn't long before they were back. Hawke tried to ignore them but the overpowering scent of roses was ruining his concentration.

'Is that you?' he asked Spike.

'Yes, it's quite nice isn't it, your Mum said

she'd got just the thing to get paint off and it worked.'

'Bet she didn't tell you she was going use perfume, did she?'

'No, but it's nice, I like the smell of roses.'

'Well I don't so you can go and sit over there, as far away from me as possible and hope the bees don't mistake you for a bunch of flowers. I'm trying to think.'

Spike sat on the grass at the bottom of the garden and leant his back against the tree.

'Have you thought of a name yet Hawke?'

'A name for what?' asked Sebastian.

'To put on the new den,' explained Spike.

Hawke sighed and scowled.

'Can't you two be quiet, I'm trying to think.'

Spike suddenly jumped up.

'I've got an idea Hawke, we could be *The Hole In The Wall Gang.*'

'It's been done,' explained Sebastian, 'that was

The Sundance Kid, Butch Cassidy, Kid Curry…'

'Don't encourage him,' interrupted Hawke, 'once he gets started he never stops. Anyway, we haven't got a wall, it's a fence.'

Spike shrugged his shoulders.

'*The Hole In The Fence Gang* then.'

'That's not been done before,' Sebastian informed them.

'We're not using that name either,' growled Hawke.

'Can't see why not if it's not been done before,' added Spike.

'Our Dad says we're not allowed to be in a gang,' explained Sebastian, 'but it's a good name.'

'No it's not,' Hawke shouted, 'we're not using it because we're going to be called *Hawke & Co.* and that's an end to it.'

There was silence. Hawke glowered at them so neither of them would argue. Spike repeated the name to himself then looked puzzled.

'If you're Hawke does that mean I'm the *Co* bit?'

'I should be in the *Co* too,' added Sebastian.

'But that'd be *Co-Co*; I don't want to be named after no clown!' replied Spike.

'Or a drink!' laughed Sebastian.

'Stop it!' yelled Hawke and looked angrily at them both.

'It's just going to be Hawke & Co, there's not going to be any Co-Co because it's just going be me and Spike, you're not in our gang.'

Hawke folded his arms and glowered at Sebastian.

'You're not allowed a gang, I'll tell.'

'If you do, you'll not be allowed in the new den.'

'Will so, Mum says we have to share everything, half the new den will be mine so you might as well let me be in Hawke & Co. then we can use all of it.'

'Never!' shouted Hawke even though he knew there was no point arguing; his parents would make him share the new den but it didn't stop him feeling annoyed.

'If you don't share I'll tell Mum and Dad what really happened to the shed,' Sebastian replied smugly.

'Why do I have to be called Co,' muttered Spike, 'why can't it be Hawke and Spike?'

'It can only be my name because I'm in charge.'

As Hawke and Spike walked up the garden, Sebastian ran past, then turned and shouted at Hawke.

'Bet you don't even know what Co. means.'

'What does it mean Hawke?' asked Spike.

'Never you mind,' replied Hawke sharply.

Hawke knew it was a great name. He'd paint it in big black capital letters on a piece of wood and hang it right above the door where everyone could see it.

Tomorrow couldn't come fast enough.

3

The New Den

Hawke watched the road below from his bedroom window. Just before eleven o'clock a big green van turned into the avenue. This was it, the moment he'd been waiting for. He waited until the doorbell rang then raced downstairs.

'You'll need to bring it down the side of the house,' Hawke's Dad told the two men who were standing at the door, 'it's going at the bottom of the garden near the tree.'

'*A real den at last,*' thought Hawke as he ran

through the kitchen and out into the garden. He'd told Spike to come round after dinner; by then he'd be ready to show it off.

'Don't get in the way,' Hawke's Dad shouted after him.

He went and sat on the kitchen step but there wasn't much to see; the two deliverymen, one old and one young, seemed to be taking ages getting the boxes out of the van.

'Lunchtime,' Hawke's Mum announced.

'I'll have mine here,' Hawke replied.

'You'll have it at the table with everyone else,' Dad shouted back.

Reluctantly Hawke went in. Didn't his Mum and Dad realise that food was the last thing on his mind? He'd far more important things to think about. He knew there wasn't any point bolting his dinner, he'd not be allowed to leave the table until everyone had finished and Sebastian always ate slowly.

After lunch Hawke ran ahead into the garden closely followed by Sebastian. They both came to an abrupt halt.

'Noooo,' cried Hawke.

At the bottom of the garden, on a raised platform, stood a yellow house with a red roof. The steps from the grass were lime green; two large red flowers had been painted on each of the walls. Sebastian started to laugh. Hawke marched down to the deliverymen.

'This isn't right.'

'It's what we've got down to deliver.'

'But it's a Wendy House, it's for girls.'

Sebastian folded his arms and turned his back on the deliverymen.

'I'm sure your little sister will love it,' the older deliveryman replied as he nodded and smiled at Sebastian.

Now it was Hawke's turn to laugh.

'That's my little brother.'

Sebastian folded his arms and turned his back on the deliverymen.

'Where's my den?' Hawke demanded.

'Our den,' corrected Sebastian.

'This is the only one we've got and it's all yours now because we've finished.'

Hawke could see his Dad coming out of the kitchen.

'Would either of you like a cup of tea?'

'No thanks, we'd better be getting off for our lunch,' the older man replied.

'What do you think to your new den?' Dad asked as he turned towards Hawke and Sebastian.

'It's a Wendy House,' was all Hawke could say.

Sebastian said nothing, he was still cross the deliveryman had mistaken him for a girl.

'It was a real bargain,' continued Dad, 'a bit of paint here and there and you'll soon have it the way you want it.'

Dad turned his attention back to the deliverymen.

'Thanks, that's a great job, I'm sure the boys will have hours of fun using it.'

Hawke wasn't so sure; the last few minutes hadn't been much fun. After all the anticipation and excitement, what a let down. Sebastian didn't look as if he was very happy either. The only one looking pleased was Dad.

'If you two let me know what you want from the DIY shop I'll go over to the retail park tomorrow; better still you can come with me and help carry it all.'

Hawke sank to his knees.

'Thanks Dad,' he whispered.

'Yes, thanks,' agreed Sebastian.

They both stared dismally at the brightly painted house. It wasn't what Hawke had envisaged at all. Then he remembered Spike was coming round. He had to stop him. He couldn't allow anyone to see this, not even Spike. He sprang to his feet.

'I've got to ring Spike.'

'No need I'm here,' a familiar voice said from behind.

Hawke glowered at Spike so he'd know not to laugh.

'Wow!' he exclaimed, 'It's a bit bright!'

'It's a Wendy House,' explained Sebastian.

'I thought you said you were having a den?'

'This is our den,' replied Hawke.

'No!' exclaimed Spike.

'Yes!' replied Hawke and Sebastian together.

There was a deathly silence as they looked at the brightly coloured house.

'Why don't we make a list of the things we want to do to it,' suggested Sebastian.

'I can only think of one thing I'd like to do but we'd need to build another ballista first,' grumbled Hawke.

Spike scrunched his eyes and looked hard at the Wendy House.

'It'd make a great observation post, you know, like the army have; the ones they paint in green and brown.'

'Camouflage,' Sebastian informed him.

'That might not be such a bad idea,' said Hawke as he also squinted at the Wendy House trying to blot out the bright colours.

'We could have a scramble net from the roof and put leaves and twigs in it too,' enthused Sebastian.

'We could,' agreed Hawke, 'I want you both to take an oath of secrecy, no one, absolutely no one, must ever know our den started out as a Wendy House.'

Spike and Sebastian exchanged looks, and then nodded in agreement.

It was then Mum called them from the kitchen doorway. As Hawke turned around he saw two children at the top of the garden waving at them.

'Tom and Sam from next door have come to say hello,' explained Mum, 'you can show them your new den.'

Hawke glowered and thrust his hands on his hips as the twins, identically dressed in tracksuits and trainers, walked towards them.

'I'm Tom and this is Sam.'

There was a tittering from Sam, and then Tom began to laugh too.

'Is this your new den?'

The tittering from Sam grew into a burst of laughter.

'Stop that now or I'll set Spike on you,' Hawke shouted.

'Hawke,' whispered Spike, 'that's not a good idea.'

Hawke didn't take any notice even though Spike looked really worried.

'If you can't be civil then go home,' said Sebastian.

The two new neighbours roared with laughter again.

'That's it, you've asked for it,' Hawke shouted, 'Spike, use your judo.'

Spike frowned at Hawke.

'You said it was to be our secret, about my judo.'

'I said it was our secret weapon, now go and sort them out.'

'I can't Hawke; I've been trying to tell you. He's not a boy.' Spike said as he pointed at Sam. 'He's a girl and you don't want to mess with her.'

'That's not a girl,' laughed Hawke.

'You couldn't be more wrong,' replied Sam.

'I told you Hawke, I've seen her at judo, she's really good, she's a green belt and you don't want to mess with her, she'll twist you around and rearrange you so your head's sticking out of your bum!'

Hawke ignored Spike. He'd weighed up the odds; there were three of them against a weedy boy and a girl.

'We can deal with this, you get him and I'll sort her out.'

Hawke took one step towards Sam. There was a loud splat; suddenly he was on his back looking up at the sky.

'I told you,' said Spike as he offered Hawke a hand to get up.

'Wow!' said Sebastian, 'that was great.'

'It was nothing,' admitted Sam, 'just a basic move.'

'You were lucky that time,' groaned Hawke as he got to his feet and lunged towards Sam again.

Wallop! Bang! Slap!

Sam did a move Spike had never seen before. Hawke seemed to whiz around in mid-air before being thrown onto the grass, only this time he wasn't looking at the sky; he was face down with Sam's foot on his bottom.

'Double wow!' gasped Sebastian. 'Can you do that Spike?'

'Nope, I can only do two basic throws.'

'Can I get up now?' demanded Hawke who was still trapped under Sam's foot.

'Not until you say sorry.'

'Me! For what?'

'For calling me a boy and for trying to attack me.'

Sebastian nodded and turned to Sam.

'I get mistaken for a girl all the time.'

Hawke groaned.

'Ok, I'm sorry, but I think you should both apologise too.'

'Why?' asked Tom.

'For being so rude and laughing at other people's misfortune,' replied Sebastian.

'Yeh, for that,' agreed Hawke, 'and for nearly poking my eye out and calling me an oik.'

There was silence whilst the twins looked at each other.

'OK,' replied Tom, 'I'm sorry I laughed at your new den.

'Me too,' said Sam, 'but I think it's great; can I look inside?'

Hawke couldn't decide if she was joking or not but he wasn't about to say anything else to provoke her into action.

'We'll invite you round when it's been converted,' said Sebastian.

'We will?' Hawke gasped as he glowered at his brother.

'That would be great,' the twins replied together.

'We'd better be going now,' explained Tom, 'we only came to say hello.'

'You still haven't introduced yourselves,' said Sam.

'I'm Sebastian and this is my brother Val…'

Hawke elbowed Sebastian out of the way before he could finish.

'I'm Hawke and this is Spike.'

'Well we'll see you again,' replied Tom.

'Oh we will,' said Hawke.

When the twins had gone Hawke turned to the other two.

'It's definitely war now, they still didn't apologise for assaulting me and calling me names, are we all agreed?'

'Agreed,' replied Spike, 'but I don't know how we'll ever be able to get the better of Sam.

'We'll use guerrilla warfare,' explained Hawke.

'I'm not dressing up as no gorilla,' cried Spike.

Sebastian laughed.

'You won't have to it doesn't mean that. It's when you do things and keep hidden, like going behind enemy lines.'

'So no gorillas?'

'No,' Hawke replied, 'are you with us little brother?'

'Does that mean I'll be in Hawke & Co.?'

'No it does not, you'll have to do something absolutely brilliant to join us but you can be a temporary member for now.'

'I could make a list of everything we'll need from the DIY store.'

Hawke smiled, Sebastian would save him a lot of time; he was good at planning.

'It'll have to be a spectacular list.'

'It will be.'

Hawke watched as Sebastian went back to the house, he'd let him make the list but if his little brother thought it was going to be that easy to be in Hawke & Co. he was mistaken.

Hawke put on his serious face so Spike would know, what he was about to say, was very important.

'We've got to make this the best den ever.'

Spike nodded in agreement.

'Can we keep the red flowers?'

'No we can't,' Hawke yelled as he climbed the lime green stairs and disappeared inside the Wendy House to think.

4

The Alterations Begin

Hawke watched as Sebastian laid out all the things they'd got from the Retail Park in front of the new den. There was paint, brushes, screws, nails and various others things, which hadn't been on their list and Dad thought they might need. Now they could begin to convert the Wendy House into the Command Bunker and Observation Post of Hawke & Co. He was wondering where they should begin when Spike arrived struggling to carry a large packing crate.

'I couldn't carry it all.'

'What you got there?' asked Hawke.

'There's a cargo net my Uncle said we could

have and a lot of other stuff too. He's been clearing out his warehouse. I've got loads more at home.'

'The net's really cool,' said Hawke as he pulled it out of the crate.

'I'll help you get the rest,' Sebastian offered.

'We'll all go,' replied Hawke. He didn't want to miss out on the pop and biscuits Spike's Mum always brought out; it was something his Mum didn't allow them to have. All they got at home was fresh fruit, nuts and pure juice, none of which Hawke particularly liked; Mum made sure they always had their *five a day*.

'We're just going round to Spike's to get some stuff,' Hawke shouted to his mum as they passed the kitchen.

Spike's house was in the next street. Hawke and Sebastian waited in front of the garage while Spike went inside and got the key. He opened the double doors wide and proudly showed them his stash.

'Wow!' exclaimed Hawke, 'this is great.'

Spike's Mum appeared at the door.

'Hello Mrs. Pike,' Sebastian said in his sweetest voice, 'we've come to help Stephen carry the rest of this round to our new den.'

'That's kind, Stephen's Dad will be pleased to get it out of the garage. You'll be wanting a drink and some biscuits before you go, it's thirsty work carrying big crates like that around.'

'We're not al…' began Sebastian before he got poked in the ribs by Hawke.

'That would be great Mrs. Pike,' said Hawke.

Three large glasses of ginger beer came out on a tray with a whole plate of chocolate biscuits. Sebastian drank and ate his share with the others.

'If you tell Mum,' said Hawke, 'I'll tell her you ate them too.'

Sebastian drank and ate his share with the others.

'There's a big difference between me eating them and you,' replied Sebastian, 'I was only being polite, you were enjoying yourself.'

Hawke raised his eyes to heaven; his little brother had an answer for everything.

When they'd finished, they thanked Spike's mum then loaded the second cargo net and everything else into two more packing crates. Spike carried one whilst Hawke and Sebastian struggled with the other between them.

'Are we allowed to keep the packing crates too?' Hawke asked Spike.

'Yep,'

'Ah double cool.'

When they were back in the garden they spread everything out on the grass and Hawke sat down to think. They needed a plan of action, he was sure they ought to do things in the right order. He was just about to ask Spike for a pad and pen when Sebastian pulled out a neatly folded piece of paper from his pocket.

'I've made a list of the things we need to do and the order we need to do them in.'

Hawke ripped the paper out of Sebastian's hand.

'I'm in charge here, I'm the one who makes all the decisions, isn't that right Spike?'

'It is Hawke, you're the one who gives all the orders.'

Sebastian looked annoyed but before he could argue he was called inside for his piano practice. Hawke sniggered; they'd have an hour to get things organized before Sebastian came back. He looked at the list. It would have taken him ages to think of all the things Sebastian had written down.

'OK, let's get going, number one, remove the window box.'

A large wooden window box was hooked onto the balcony. Hawke went up the steps and leant over to unhook it whilst Spike stayed on the grass and supported it from underneath. As he lowered it down he had a great idea.

'We could use this as a bench if we turned it upside down.'

Spike nodded.

'What about using the crates as a table?

'That's not such a bad idea, if we put them together on their sides we could get Dad to put some shelves inside too.'

'What's next Hawke?'

'Number two, paint the roof.'

By the time Sebastian came back, the roof was olive green. Hawke and Spike were half way round the walls.

'Can I help?'

'No, Mum and Dad wouldn't like it.'

'That's not fair, it was my list, they'd say I could, I know they would, I want to paint too.'

'Ok, grab a brush, we'll carry on up here, the sooner we get rid of that revolting yellow and those awful red flowers the better.'

'I like the flowers,' mumbled Spike.

'But they wouldn't look good on the side of a Command Bunker and Observation Post,' replied Hawke, 'and I'm not going to give either of those two next door any reason to laugh at us again. There isn't any room for you to come up here so you can paint the stilts and the back of the ladder only do it properly so there aren't any gaps.'

Sebastian picked up a tin of olive green paint and whistled cheerfully as he painted.

By lunchtime they'd finished painting.

'You two are a right mess,' said Sebastian as Hawke and Spike joined him on the grass, 'I've been really careful, I haven't got any on myself.'

Hawke laughed. 'That's what you think, you should see your hair!'

'What's wrong with my hair?'

'It's all green on top,' explained Spike, 'it looks like you got a great big cow pat on your head.'

'Oh no, Mum will kill me.'

When they went in for dinner their Mum wasn't pleased.

'You're not going out there again until Valentine and Stephen have finished,' she told Sebastian crossly, 'you're going upstairs to have your hair washed.'

Hawke smiled to himself.

After lunch, Hawke and Spike stood for a few moments admiring their morning's work. They could hear Sebastian's cries as his Mum tried to scrub the paint out of his beautiful blonde curls. For the rest of the afternoon Hawke felt smug, not only had Sebastian been in trouble but he'd also been banned from helping until the Command Bunker was finished. Hawke thought he could keep his little brother away for at least a week; they'd still got all the camouflage to sort out. He opened the not so neatly folded piece of paper and consulted the list to see what needed to be done next.

5

The Command Bunker

By the end of the week the Command Bunker of Hawke & Co. looked great. The olive green paint, now daubed with brown and black, gave it a real camouflage look. All the bright colours of the Wendy House were gone. Dad fixed one of the cargo nets to the top of the Bunker and it was now draped over the balcony. The sign saying *HAWKE & CO.* had been hung on the door. They'd made good use of the space under the stilts. Dad had put some decking on the grass, covered it with a ground sheet and then laid the carpet, which they'd salvaged from the old shed, over the top. On three of the open sides they'd nailed the rest of the groundsheets to the stilts as a windbreak. Spike's uncle had given him some half empty sand bags; these were now around the bottom of the new groundsheet walls to stop them flapping about if it got windy.

Hawke and Spike were in the process of threading branches and grass through the holes in the second cargo net, which they intended to throw over the roof, when Sebastian joined them.

Hawke smiled to himself when saw the faint tinge of olive-green still on the top of Sebastian's head.

'It looks great, I wish Mum had let me help.'

'Well she didn't so tough.'

'It's not finished yet,' added Spike.

'What you going to do in the room downstairs?'

'Der... I thought you were the brainy one

little bro… it's an observation post.'

'To observe what, all you'll see from there is the grass growing!'

Hawke glowered at Sebastian; he'd been so desperate to transform the Wendy House he'd not realized they wouldn't be able to spy on the next-door neighbours from a bunker on the ground.

'It's where we're going to observe our plans, see, we've got a table and a bench.'

'You'd be better off lying on this side of the roof if you want to see over into Tom and Sam's garden,' continued Sebastian.

'I know, I know, don't you think I've already worked that out, it's all in hand little brother.'

'Mum says we can have the old washing line pole, she doesn't need it now she's got a rotary dryer.'

'It's a rusty old pole, what we going do with that?

'Fly our flag from it,' replied Sebastian

triumphantly as he produced a piece of cloth.

Hawke and Spike watched as Sebastian laid the cloth on the grass and unfolded it carefully. It was white with a black silhouette of a hawk painted onto it.

Spike slapped Sebastian on the back.

'It's cool, I wish I could draw like that.'

'He's only traced it.'

'I didn't, I copied it out of my Book of British Birds.'

'Same thing.'

'It's not… Mum said it's really good.'

'She would.'

'Don't you like it?'

'If you want that flag up you're going to have to sort that pole out yourself, I'm not scraping all that rust off.'

'No need, Dad's sorted it out already… does it mean I can be in Hawke & Co now?'

Sebastian laid the cloth on the grass and
unfolded it carefully.

'No it does not, you're going to have to do something better than slapping a bit of paint on a bit of material to join us.'

Spike knelt down and examined the flag closely.

'I think it's a great hawk, he's painted it really well and all the edges have been sewn; it'll make a great flag.'

'No one asked you... anyway... I'm in charge. I think we should have it over there by the corner. Spike go and stand over there, and Sebastian, you can go and tell Dad we're ready for him to put the flagpole up.'

The next afternoon the two members and one honorary member of Hawke & Co. met at the Command Bunker. Sebastian and Spike stood admiring the new flagpole.

'It's a shame there isn't any breeze today,' said Sebastian.

'Why don't we get your Dad to fix a bit of wood from the top and then we could hang it down and you'd always be able to see it.'

'It wouldn't be a flag then would it, besides, it looks OK the way it is.'

Hawke stood with the door open.

'Are you two ready now? Can we all go inside and start the meeting?'

Once they were upstairs, Spike and Sebastian admired the new bench, which had once been the window box on the Wendy House. It looked better now it was painted green and had a long cushion on top.

'Come on you two, gather round,' snapped Hawke as he took the lid from a thick marker pen and bent over a large piece of paper he'd spread out on top of the table.

'We need to make a plan of action.'

'What's the table and bench doing up here Hawke? I thought you said we were going to use the observation bunker downstairs for plans?' said Spike.

'We are when we've made them, but first we have to write them out and we do that in our HQ so we need the table up here, see.'

'What's an HQ Hawke?'

'It's an abbreviation for Headquarters,' explained Sebastian, 'just like Co. is a short way of saying 'company'.

'Wow!' exclaimed Spike, 'does that mean we're in business and got our very own company?'

'It means,' began Hawke feeling quite exasperated, 'we're a *company* of soldiers and we are at war with those snobby kids next door and this is our Headquarters where we're going to plan out just how we're going to teach them a lesson.'

'I don't think they're snobby,' replied Sebastian.

'Well you wouldn't, anyone who's proud of having a name like Sebastian Amadeus wouldn't think anyone was snobby.'

'It's not my fault you don't like your name.'

'I don't like my name either,' sighed Spike.

'Stephen isn't as bad as Valentine,' replied Hawke.

'It's not Stephen I'm bothered about, it's the Pike bit.'

'But it's your name, you wouldn't be called Spike if you had a different one,' explained Hawke, 'If your surname was Potts we'd put the S in front of it and call you Spots and that really wouldn't be cool.'

'Platt, Peck or Pook wouldn't be too good either,' laughed Sebastian.

Spike wrote down the names Hawke and Sebastian had suggested at the bottom of Hawke's large piece of paper. He put a capital 'S' in front of them all.

SPOTTS

SPLATT SPOOK

SPECK

SPIKE

'Maybe Pike's not so bad after all.'

Hawke sighed.

'If we've all finished discussing names can we get on?'

A shout from the kitchen put an abrupt end to the first meeting of Hawke & Co. They were both called in for tea, which meant Spike needed to go home for his too.

Hawke sighed as he replaced the lid on the marker pen, the planning would have to wait for another day, at least the Command Bunker was finished, even if the Observation Post still needed a bit of sorting out.

6

The Summer Fete

'I don't want to go!' wailed Hawke.

'We're all going dear,' explained his mother, 'we're a family and this is something we do together.'

'But I'm not musical like the rest of you so I shouldn't have to go,' continued Hawke even though he knew he was on a loser. He would be made to go no matter what; today was the village Summer Fete and every year his family performed for an hour as *Hawke's Nest*. His Mum and Dad both played guitars, Sebastian accompanied them on the keyboard and all three of them sang. Hawke couldn't play any instrument, even the shaker he was given never sounded right. His mother would smile encouragingly and his Dad would signal the beat for him to follow, but he rarely got it right. The only good thing was they never expected him to sing; he was grateful for that.

It was the one day of the year he hated, it was pure torture to be up on the stage with everyone staring. Not only that but Mum insisted the family wore matching green tabards and felt hats which had a single feather in them. Dad said they were real hawk's feathers but Sebastian told him they were from a pheasant. It didn't matter to Hawke what kind of feather it was, he just felt stupid in the outfit and what's more he was expected to smile and at least look as if he was enjoying himself.

'Put it on,' Mum told him as she produced the dreaded hat.

'When we get there,' Hawke grumbled. He

looked dismally at it then frowned at Sebastian who was admiring himself in the mirror.

'Come on Valentine, Dad's nearly finished loading the car, we're going to have a great time.'

'We are,' agreed Sebastian, 'I've been looking forward to this all week.'

Hawke said nothing and just stared glumly at the hat he was holding.

'Is everyone ready?' Dad shouted from the gate, 'we don't want to be late.'

On the way Mum read out the order of songs they'd be playing. It wasn't long before they arrived at Spout Farm. Dad turned the car into the field next to the farmhouse. There were lots of people already there.

Hawke said nothing.

Hawke looked out of the back window and to his horror saw their next-door neighbours in the car behind. Sebastian had seen them too and started waving.

'Ooh look! I think Tom and Sam are going to the Fete too with their Mum and Dad.'

'Ah great!' grumbled Hawke, 'that's all I need.' How was anyone ever going to take him seriously as the leader of Hawke & Co. when he was forced to dress up like Robin Hood?

The twins waved back to Sebastian; Hawke ignored them.

Whilst Mum and Dad set up the stands, microphones and keyboard, Hawke and Sebastian were allowed to have a quick look around the Fete. They saw the twins in the distance, Sam was dressed in her white judo suit and Tom was carrying an old suitcase. Hawke remembered Spike telling him there was going to be a judo demonstration at the Fete, with any luck it might be on at the same time as *Hawke's Nest* then the twins wouldn't see him making a fool of himself.

'Hawke, over here,' came a loud voice from behind.

Hawke looked round, Spike was running towards the roped off area.

'We're doing our demonstration first, you'll be able to watch us, then I'll come and see you playing.'

'It's OK, you don't have to come and watch me, it'll be the same as last year, I haven't improved.'

'Oh but I want to come and watch, I like the songs and you all look great in your outfits.'

Hawke glowered at Spike.

'See,' said Sebastian, 'I told you we looked good.'

There was an ear-piercing screech from the microphone as someone from the Fete Committee gave it a tap. All the important people climbed the steps onto the stage and the Fete was officially opened; the first event was announced. Spike ducked under the roped off area and joined the rest of his judo group. Hawke cringed as he heard the announcement that *Hawke's Nest* would be on the main stage after the judo. Why did they have to be where everyone would see them, why couldn't they play at the back of the field? Why did they have to play at all?

Hawke went to join Sebastian and the judo began. Sebastian was in awe as Sam demonstrated her skills; he clapped enthusiastically each time she threw someone to the floor. Hawke only had one thing on his mind, how to avoid being seen by anyone he knew. It wasn't going to be easy, most people knew him in the village, when both your parents are teachers and your little brother is a gifted musician, it's hard not to be recognized.

'A big round of applause for the volunteers who have just given us an amazing demonstration of their judo skills...' said the crackly voice from the loud speakers. '...and now, if you'd like to make your way to the centre stage, Hawke's Nest will be performing shortly.'

'That's us,' said Sebastian as he nudged Hawke.

'I know.'

'You'd better put your costume on.'

'Not until I have to.'

Sebastian hurried off.

When Hawke arrived behind the centre stage he reluctantly put the green tabard on; he pulled the felt hat down over his ears.

'What have you done to your outfit?' Mum said as she gasped in horror.

Hawke had stuffed the tabard into the hat whilst they'd been watching the judo and tucked it all under his arm. It was now very creased and what was worse, he'd lost the feather out of his hat. His Mum looked really cross.

'You'd better stand at the back, I can't have people seeing you looking all crumpled.'

Hawke actually smiled. This was an unexpected turn in events. He'd been ordered to keep out of sight and at the end of their performance he'd be able to escape quickly off the back of the stage. He pulled the hat even lower to cover his face. Dad played the introduction to the first song and

Hawke tried to keep the beat with his shaker, in what he hoped was the right places. There was quite a crowd around the stage and Hawke could see Spike clapping and singing along with the rest. A group of girls had gathered as close to the front as they could, but for once this didn't bother Hawke, he was keeping well out of sight. The less he had to do with girls the better.

After the last song the crowd called out for more. Dad announced Sebastian would entertain them with a solo. This was a brilliant stroke of luck, Hawke wriggled out of his outfit and left it by the curtain then jumped off the back of the stage. There was a resounding crack as Hawke's right foot landed inside an open suitcase.

'Oh no! Look what you've done!' someone shouted at him.

Hawke looked down at his foot. He'd landed on top of a ventriloquist's dummy. Mum had moved to the back of the stage and was frowning at him holding a finger to her lips as a signal for quiet whilst Sebastian was performing. Hawke turned around to see who'd spoken and came face to face with Tom. He could see he was very angry.

'I'm sorry,' he whispered, 'I didn't expect anything to be there, it was an accident.'

'What am I going to do? I'm supposed to be on next.'

'Shhh!' said Mum frowning at both of them now.

'We've got some tape Dad uses to stick the cables down to the floor so no one trips up,' offered Hawke in the smallest whisper he could manage.

'That's not going to help, he's ruined.'

There was thunderous applause from the audience and seconds later Hawke's Mum was in front of them both with her hands on her hips looking really cross.

'It wasn't very kind to speak through Sebastian's solo, what is the matter with you both?'

Tom looked accusingly at Hawke then pointed towards the broken dummy.

'He broke Alfred.'

'I didn't do it on purpose Mum, it was an accident.'

Hawke's Mum bent down and examined the dummy.

'We're going to have to help Tom out. If your Dad takes his time packing up the instruments I think I'll have just enough time to work something out. Don't worry Tom, we'll get you on stage.'

Mum didn't explain what she had in mind but Hawke was sure he wasn't going to like whatever it was.

7

The Performance

Hawke frowned as Tom bowed to the crowd. He watched from the side of the stage as Tom adjusted the microphone and re-positioned the chair, which had been placed on the stage for him. Tom then turned and walked straight towards Hawke, grabbed him by the back of the tight jacket he'd been squeezed into and marched him back to the chair.

'I'd like to introduce you to Alfred,' Tom began, 'give him a wave.'

The crowd obligingly waved to the dummy as Tom sat down on the chair and dragged Hawke onto his knee. Hawke flinched; it had been bad enough wearing the Robin Hood outfit but his Mum had made him put all the dummy's clothes on. Now he was perched on Tom's knee pretending to be Alfred, the talking elf! He kept his head down; the red hat with the bell on the end was draped over his face. How was he ever going to live this one down? If anyone recognized him he'd be ridiculed forever.

'Let's see if Alfred will wave back,' said Tom giving Hawke a thump in the small of his back as his cue to wave to everyone.

Hawke raised his hand slowly and gave a jerky wave without raising his head. The bells on his collar jingled.

'Don't be shy,' coaxed Tom, 'how about a smile too.'

Hawke shook his head and sent the bell ringing. There was no way he was looking at the crowd. His Mum had used her bright red lipstick, to make circles on his cheeks. She'd drawn on his

Mum had made him put all the dummy's clothes on.

mouth with a black marker pen, to make it look hinged and given him bright red lips too.

'Don't you want to say hello to everyone?' continued Tom.

Hawke shook his head so violently he nearly lost the hat. He'd have to be more careful; the hat was the only thing keeping his identity a secret. He felt ridiculous in the small green shorts, striped socks and red jacket. The only thing keeping everything together was a belt. Only his shoes belonged to him; if his Mum had managed to squeeze his feet into Alfred's green felt slippers, he'd have bells on his feet too.

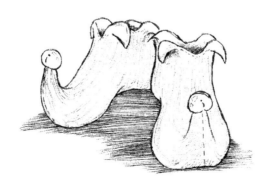

He could see Sam at the front giggling. She whispered something to Sebastian, which made him grin; both of them were looking straight at him and he knew his secret was out.

For the next twenty minutes Tom went through his rehearsed routine. He thumped Hawke in the back each time he wanted him to open and shut his mouth. Hawke felt more like a goldfish than a ventriloquist's dummy.

'We're going to finish with a song,' Tom announced.

By this time Hawke was completely fed up; since nothing was going to improve his situation he decided to join in with the singing. He could tell Tom wasn't pleased and from the punches he kept getting in his back, he knew he was getting his own back.

Hawke's voice was dreadful and the duet with Tom started the whole crowd laughing. When they'd finished, Tom pushed Hawke on the shoulder, to make him bow. The crowd cheered and clapped; even more than they had for Sebastian's solo. It seemed they'd been a great success but once they'd left the stage and were out of sight, Tom began shouting at Hawke.

'You ruined my act; first you broke Alfred, then you wouldn't look at the audience and worse still you spoilt my song. Why on earth did you join in when you can't sing?'

'I wasn't exactly enjoying myself up there you know,' exploded Hawke.

Tom clenched his fist and swiped at Hawke narrowly missing his nose.

'That's enough you two,' interrupted Hawke's Mum as she came backstage, Sam and Sebastian followed her; both were grinning.

Hawke frowned and waited for them to start making fun of him; instead they came over and congratulated him.

'You were fantastic,' said Sam.

'Absolutely brilliant,' agreed Sebastian.

'You were great too Tom, Mum says you should forget about the dummy and use Valentine instead.'

'No way,' yelled Hawke and Tom together.

Hawke glowered at Sam; she'd said Valentine so sweetly he just knew she was doing it to annoy him.

'Well the crowd loved you too,' said Hawke's Mum, 'you made a brilliant elf Valentine.'

There was that name again, Sam and Mrs Hawke both smiled at each other.

'Is it too much to ask for a bit of privacy so I can get changed?' Hawke grumbled. He couldn't wait to get out of the elf costume.

Sam and Mrs Hawke closed the curtain as

they left the back stage area.

'I'd like you to disappear too,' continued Hawke as he looked crossly at Sebastian and Tom.

'No way, not until I get Alfred's clothes back,' Tom shouted.

'You don't think I want to keep them do you?'

Just then Spike came through the curtain and put his arms round both their shoulders.

'You two were great!'

'Go away,' sulked Hawke.

'He broke Alfred,' said Tom pointing towards the bare dummy.

'You mean, you didn't, you hadn't…' replied Spike.

'No we hadn't practiced it and we certainly ARE'NT ever doing it again,' shouted Hawke.

'Ah, what a shame, I really enjoyed it.'

'So did I,' agreed Sebastian.

'I thought I told you to disappear,' Hawke growled as he glowered at his younger brother.

'You did, but Mum says we can go round the rest of the Fete when you've changed so I'm waiting for you.'

'Well you're just going to have to go and find Mum because when I get this stuff of my face I want to go home.'

Hawke felt cross, he didn't see why he should have to look after his little brother all afternoon whilst his Mum and Dad sat chatting with their friends.

Tom put what was left of Alfred away in the bottom of the suitcase and laid the elf costume carefully on top. Neither he nor Hawke said a word to each other. Once he had his own clothes on, Hawke made his way to the toilets and tried to wash the lipstick and black marker pen off. To his horror it wouldn't go. The lipstick left two livid pink patches, which looked like he'd been stung on each cheek. His nose glowed like a beacon. The black ink had faded a bit, but his lips and chin were very red, from where he'd been rubbing them.

'Hurry up Valentine,' Hawke's Mum called from the other side of the washroom door, 'Sebastian's been waiting ages for you.'

'I want to go home.'

'Not until we're all ready.'

'But I can't go round the Fete like this.'

Hawke opened the washroom door.

'A bit of soap and water will get rid of that.'

'It won't Mum, I've already tried.'

Spike and Sebastian arrived; Hawke frowned at them both so they wouldn't say anything.

'I'll take Sebastian round the Fete Mrs Hawke,' offered Spike.

'How kind Stephen; that would be lovely.'

Hawke watched Spike and Sebastian race off

in the direction of the Bouncy Castle.

'Why don't you go after them?' his Mum said kindly.

Hawke didn't reply.

For the next two hours Hawke sat and sulked in the car. He was really cross with his Mum. How could she have made him wear the elf outfit? He hadn't broken Alfred on purpose. He had to work out a plan to get back at Tom and Sam, he almost included Spike and Sebastian too, but he knew he'd need them to help with whatever he thought of.

Eventually he saw his Mum, Dad, Sebastian and Spike with their arms full of equipment as they made their way back to the car.

'You should have come,' said Spike, 'it was great fun, Sebastian won six prizes and I got a coconut.'

Hawke looked at their happy faces.

'I hate Fete day,' he grumbled to himself.

8

The Master Plan

Hawke was upstairs in the Command Bunker putting the finishing touches to his master plan, whilst he waited for Spike to arrive. He was going to wipe the smile off Sam's face and make Tom feel as annoyed as he'd done yesterday at the Fete.

When Hawke saw Spike in the garden he shouted down to him from the Bunker.

'I'm here, come on up.'

'Did you know there's a gang of girls hanging around your front gate?'

'What do they want?'

'I don't know, don't talk to girls, but they must be going to write something because they've all got pads and pens.'

'Let's have a look from my bedroom window, we'll be safe there and can see what they're up to.'

They raced back to the house and went upstairs to the room Hawke shared with Sebastian. It was a sore point he'd got to share a room with his little brother even if it was the biggest bedroom. Hawke moved the net curtain a fraction so he could see what was going on. One of the girls saw the curtain move and pointed excitedly at the window. Seven eager faces looked up in expectation.

'It's him,' squealed one of them.

'Hi,' shouted another and started to wave.

'What do they want Hawke?'

'How do I know?'

Hawke suspected the girls might want his autograph after his performance yesterday.

Everyone kept telling him what a brilliant elf he'd been. His suspicions were confirmed when his Mum shouted upstairs.

'Your fan club's outside waiting for your autograph!'

'I know,' replied Hawke and Sebastian together.

'They're waiting for me,' explained Sebastian as he entered the bedroom.

'I think not little brother, you just watch what happens when I open the window, then we'll see who they're waiting for.'

Hawke pulled back the net and opened the window. He suddenly felt embarrassed but was determined to prove to Sebastian the girls were waiting for him to appear. As the window started to open the group of girls below giggled excitedly. When they saw Hawke they began to whisper to one another.

'Is Sebastian there?' asked one.

'Ye..e..s,' stuttered Hawke.

'See,' smirked Sebastian, 'I told you they were waiting for me.'

Hawke slammed the window and turned on his heel.

'To the Bunker,' he commanded Spike.

Sebastian went off to the front garden to sign autographs whilst Hawke and Spike went back to the Bunker. They took up their positions on either side of their new table, Hawke on his thinking chair, and Spike on the bench. Together they looked at the sheet of paper, which Hawke had spread out on top.

'This is the master plan, we're going to need a bucket and two spades.'

'Are we going to dig a tunnel?' asked Spike excitedly.

'No, we're going to hunt for slugs and snails,

we're going to use the spades to pick them up and put them in the bucket.'

'What're we going to do with a bucket full of slugs and snails?'

Hawke began to laugh.

'When it's full, we're going to get through into next door's garden and put them into their pool. That should stop them splashing about and enjoying themselves, they won't like having to share it with a load of slimies.'

'They're gastropods actually,' said Sebastian who'd once again appeared from nowhere.

'*Nasty pods*?' asked Spike.

'Gas… tro… pods,' said Sebastian slowly, 'it means they only have one foot; some have shells like snails and some don't.'

'Thank you and goodbye,' said Hawke as he steered Sebastian towards the door.

'You can't make me go, Mum and Dad said you've got to share the Bunker with me, anyway,

I'll go and tell her what you're planning to do with the slugs and snails if you don't let me stay.'

Hawke sighed. He knew Sebastian was right; but maybe with his help they'd fill the bucket quicker.

'You'll need a spade,' explained Hawke.

Sebastian looked horrified.

'A spade will hurt them, you need to pick them up carefully with your fingers.'

'Not me, but you can; here, take the bucket, if you fill it we might let you join Hawke & Co.'

Sebastian looked excited and shuffled from one foot to the other.

'Do you mean it, if I fill the bucket you'll let me join?'

Hawke nodded, 'reckon so, do you agree Spike?'

Spike nodded.

Hawke chuckled to himself as Sebastian took the bucket; he was confident he'd never fill it.

Hawke and Spike watched as Sebastian skipped across the lawn.

'Right, come on Spike whilst he's busy, we've got a plank to loosen.'

'A plank?'

'Yes a plank, I've already found a loose one in the fence and if we can get two of them out we'll be able to get through into next-door's garden.'

'Won't they notice the planks are missing?'

'Not if we do it right. We'll get them off then lean then back again. Only we'll know where they are; we'll be able to move them and squeeze through when we need to.'

'That's a great plan Hawke.'

'It's a master plan, now, all we need is that bucket full of slugs and snails!'

'The *nasty pods*.' Spike informed him.

You need to pick them up carefully with your fingers.

Hawke laughed.

'They will be when those snotty kids next door find them in their pool!'

By the time Hawke and Spike had the two planks out of the fence, Sebastian returned with the bucket. Hawke carefully propped the planks back so no one would notice the gap.

'Back so soon little brother?'

'Yes, I've done what you wanted.'

Sebastian showed the bucket to Spike.

'Ugh, look Hawke, he's filled it!'

Hawke was amazed, he'd no idea how Sebastian could have found so many so soon.

'When are you going to put them in the pool Hawke?' asked Spike.

'Tonight, when everyone's asleep; won't they get a shock in the morning!'

'I think I should point out…' began Sebastian.

Hawke frowned at his little brother.

'I don't need you to point anything out, this is my master plan and tomorrow we're going to hear Sam screaming from the other side of our fence.'

Hawke put the bucket behind the Bunker, out of sight, in readiness for his midnight expedition. When he came back round to the front, Sebastian was shuffling from one foot to the other again.

'So does that mean I can be in Hawke & Co?'

'Suppose so,' replied Hawke begrudgingly, 'as long as you don't tell Mum what we're planning, remember, you're in it too now.'

'I won't say a word, I promise, but I really think you ought to know…'

'I'm in charge,' yelled Hawke, 'and when I want your opinion I'll ask for it so just do as you promised and don't say another word.'

Sebastian closed his mouth then smiled sweetly. Hawke ignored his brother, nothing was going to upset his master plan; he couldn't wait for midnight.

9

The Midnight Expedition

Hawke lay in bed; he was too excited to sleep. When the living room clock chimed twelve he pulled back the covers. Loud snores were coming from his parent's bedroom. Sebastian had been asleep for hours. He'd decided he wasn't going to change out of his pyjamas and would just put his trainers on; they were ready by the side of the bed. He moved carefully and quietly around his room, not forgetting to pick up his torch before making his way downstairs. He congratulated himself for getting to the bottom without making any sound, several of the stairs creaked badly if you trod on them in the wrong place. This wasn't the first time Hawke had sneaked downstairs after midnight. He quite often got thirsty and would go and help himself to a glass of milk; he'd have had a biscuit too if there's been any in the house.

Everything was going well. He turned the key in the kitchen door slowly, a loud click made him hold his breath, but no one stirred. A cool breeze ruffled his hair and made a shiver run down his back. Everything looked different in the dark. He took a deep breath and stepped outside then slowly closed the door. The grass was wet and by the time he was behind the Command Bunker he could feel the damp seeping through his trainers. He flicked the torch on. To his horror, the bucket, which he knew had been full of slugs and snails, was now half empty. As he shone the torch around he could see them escaping down the sides; they were all over the grass too. He took a deep breath and pulled all the snails off the outside of the bucket and popped them back in. The slug he picked up was cold and slimy. How could Sebastian have picked up so many? He looked sadly into the bucket, what he had would have to do. He couldn't go and wake Sebastian to fill the bucket again and he certainly wasn't picking any more up.

The two loose planks in the fence were easy to find. He moved them carefully aside. He didn't want to risk being seen so he switched the torch off. With the bucket securely in one hand and his torch in the other, he squeezed through the gap. He peered into the darkness; it seems a long way to where the pool was.

Next-door's garden was a jungle. Twigs cracked each time he put his foot down, no matter how careful he was. His pyjama bottoms were wet and flapped around his ankles; his trainers were making squelching sounds. He was halfway up the garden when disaster struck. His foot got caught under a root and he went head over heels into the bushes. The torch flew out of his hand and although he tried not to let go of the bucket, it shot up into the air and somersaulted before landing, upside down, on his head. He shuddered as a blob of slime slowly ran down the back of his neck. He carefully removed the bucket. Hawke cringed as he picked the slugs and snails from his hair. He used his sleeve to wipe the slime off. This certainly hadn't been a part of his master plan but he wasn't going to give up. He was still cross with the twins. He picked

He shuddered as a blob of slime
ran slowly down the back of his neck.

up the bucket, took a deep breath, then carried on through the tangle of weeds and bushes.

When he reached the pool he shook the bucket over the water. A few fell in but the rest were firmly attached to the inside. He shuddered as he scooped the rest out, handful by handful. By the time he'd finished his hand and arm was covered in slime. This was not quite the slick operation he'd thought it would be. At least he'd accomplished his mission; there were now slugs and snails in the pool. He couldn't wait to hear Sam scream when she saw them floating in the water.

By the time Hawke was back upstairs, the clock in the living room was chiming one. He crept into the bathroom and wiped his hands and face on a flannel. Almost as soon as his head hit the pillow he was asleep.

'Ugh, what's that mess!' exclaimed Sebastian.

'What mess?' Hawke replied sleepily.

'I thought you were going to put the slugs and snails in next door's pool.'

'I did.'

'It looks like you brought most of them back with you.'

'What do you mean?'

'You've been sleeping with them!'

Sebastian pointed to Hawke's pillow where two fat slugs had spent the night.

'You've got some in your hair too!'

'Help me get them out, that's an order.'

Sebastian removed three fat slugs, opened

the window and carefully put them on the windowsill.

'If you'd listened to me yesterday afternoon none of this would have happened.'

'I don't know what you're talking about, the master plan worked like a dream, leave the window open, we should be hearing the screams soon when they find their pool infested with slimies.'

Sebastian sighed.

'They're gastropods, I tried to tell you about them yesterday, there's things you needed to know.'

'Like what?'

'Like, if you don't put a lid on the bucket they'll escape, and, even if you take gastropods to another location they return to their original habitat very quickly.'

'Just tell me what you mean.'

'That none of the slugs and snails you threw

into the pool last night will still be there this morning, they'll all be back under the log pile where I found them yesterday.'

'You are joking?'

'I never joke about facts.'

'Well why didn't you tell me?'

'Because you told me not to say another word so I didn't, I was only following orders.'

Hawke sat on the end of his bed for ages; his master plan was in ruins. He shook his head; all that

work for nothing. How was he supposed to know gastropods were like homing pigeons?

He made his way to the bathroom, opened the window and stood on tiptoe to try and get a good look at the pool. Sebastian was right, there wasn't a slug or snail in sight. He was just about

How was he supposed to know gastropods
were like homing pigeons?

to shut the window when he heard Tom shout. Maybe some of the slugs and snails were in the pool after all? He held his breath.

'Look Sam,' Tom shouted triumphantly, 'look what I've found, it's a torch, and guess what, it works.'

10

The Mysterious Missile

'I wish it would stop raining,' sighed Spike.
The old beech tree creaked and groaned
as its branches were tossed around by the
wind. Occasionally a branch would thump
onto the roof of the Command Bunker where
the members of Hawke & Co. were gathered
around their packing crate table.

'It's forecast to rain all week,' said Sebastian,
'storms and gales for the next two days followed
by heavy rain.'

'But it's our summer holiday,' moaned Hawke.

'Well there's one good thing,' said Spike.

'There is?' replied Hawke.

'Tom and Sam can't use their pool, they're stuck inside.'

Hawke smiled.

'I hadn't thought about that, you're right, they'll have to stay in all week.'

'Perhaps we ought to invite them over,' Sebastian offered.

'No,' shouted Hawke, 'after what they did.'

'What did they do Hawke?' asked Spike.

'They laughed at the Command Bunker.'

'But that was when it was a Wendy House,' interrupted Sebastian, 'and I know Tom said it looks really smart now.'

'How do you know that?' snapped Hawke, 'if you've been talking to the other side you're going to have to leave the gang.'

'What else did they do?' continued Spike.

'Tom made me dress up as that elf and sit on his knee and he kept punching me in the back.'

'It was Mum who made you put the elf's clothes on, not Tom,' Sebastian pointed out.

'They never invited us to play in their pool, so why should we invite them to our Bunker…?' Hawke grumbled as he placed a clean piece of paper and a pen in front of them.

Neither Spike nor Sebastian had anything to say, both of them sat staring at the table.

'… and they still haven't apologised for calling me an oik… so I'll tell you what we're going to do, we're going to plan our next strategy. We need another plan, a brilliant one this time, one that won't fail. OK, any ideas.'

Again there was silence except for the rain beating down on the roof.

'We could play Monopoly,' suggested Sebastian.

Hawke frowned. It was more important to find a way to make the twins unhappy; wasting a couple of hours on a game of Monopoly wasn't going to get them very far, and besides, Sebastian always won. His thoughts were interrupted by a thud on the balcony. It wasn't the tree because the thud had been followed by a couple of smaller thuds, as if something had landed then rolled to a halt.

'What was that?' whispered Sebastian.

'There's something on the balcony,' Spike informed them both as he squinted through the raindrops on the windowpane.

'Something like what?' asked Hawke.

'Well, like a tin!'

Hawke opened the door to view the mysterious object. It was a round tin; two thick elastic bands secured the lid.

'Do you think it's dangerous?' asked Spike who was hiding behind Hawke.

'Well, there's only one way to find out,' replied Sebastian as he reached out and grabbed the tin then quickly put it on the table.

'Do you think it's dangerous?'

Hawke shut the door. They all gathered around the table with the wet tin in the middle. No one made a move to open it.

'I think you should open it,' suggested Spike as he turned to look at Hawke.

'No, I think he should,' replied Hawke pointing at Sebastian, 'he brought it in, so he can see what's inside.'

Sebastian carefully removed the rubber bands.

'So far so good,' he said as he breathed a sigh of relief.

As he pulled hard on the lid something rattled inside. He pulled again and eventually the lid came off. Hawke and Spike held their breath as Sebastian looked inside then he tipped a large stone onto the table.

'There's something else inside, around the inside of the tin.'

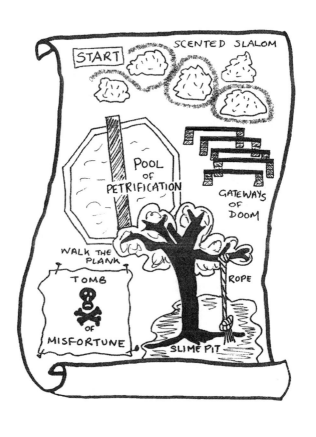

'It looks like a map!'

'Give it here,' Hawke ordered, 'I'm in charge.'

'You shouldn't throw stones,' said Sebastian.

'I think it was used to weight the tin,' replied Hawke.

'Well it could have smashed the window,' continued Sebastian.

'What's on the paper?' asked Spike.

Hawke unrolled it.

'It looks like a map!'

They all crowded around.

It was only when Hawke saw the octagonal shape in the top left hand corner, he realized it was a map of the garden next door. There were lots of other strange drawings too. Underneath the pool in capital letters someone had written *WALK THE PLANK*.

'It's an *Assault Course Challenge*,' announced Sebastian.

'What makes you think that?' asked Hawke sarcastically.

'Because it says so on the back!' smirked Sebastian.

Hawke turned the paper over.

'You're right, it's a challenge and there's a list of what we've got to do, if we accept. Look, the first one says, *Walk the plank across the Pool of Petrification.*'

'What's *Petri fi cation*?' asked Spike.

'It means you get turned to stone if you touch the water,' explained Sebastian.

'Wow!' exclaimed Spike, 'that's cool!'

'It's not real you idiot,' snapped Hawke, 'it's only pretend.'

'But it sounds like fun,' added Spike.

Hawke studied the rest of the list and then passed it over to Sebastian to read out.

'Cross the Slime Pit... Scramble through the Tomb of Misfortune... Pass through the Gateways of Doom... Slither through the Scented Slalom,'

ASSAULT
  COURSE
CHALLENGE

• Walk the plank across the Pool of Petrification...
• Cross the Slime Pit...
• Scramble through the Tomb of Misfortune...
• Pass through the Gateways of Doom...
• Slither through the Scented Slalom...

IF YOU DARE!

there's a list of what we've got to do

'It really does sound fun,' said Spike excitedly, 'let's have a look at the other side.'

Sebastian turned the paper over and spread the map out on the table. It was obviously the twin's garden and dotted around it were the challenges, which had been listed on the back.

'We've got to accept,' said Sebastian, 'it would be rude not to.'

'I don't care about rude,' snapped Hawke, 'we've got to accept or we'll lose face, they've dared us to do their stupid challenges, if we don't they'll think we're scared.'

'So does that mean we're going to accept Hawke?' asked Spike.

'Of course it does.'

'Cool!' said Spike; 'I can't wait to see the Tomb of Misfortune, how big do you think the tomb is?'

'It's not a real tomb,' snapped Hawke impatiently, 'no one has a *real tomb* in their back garden.'

Spike looked disappointed but his expression soon changed when he looked out of the window, 'It's stopped raining.'

'Looks like the forecast was wrong little brother, OK, when do they want us to do this challenge?'

Sebastian turned the map over.

'Tomorrow morning at 10 o'clock.'

'Write a reply,' ordered Hawke, 'we'll do their stupid assault course and we'll show them just how great we are.'

Sebastian took the piece of paper Hawke had placed on the table and wrote to Tom and Sam to accept their challenge. He folded the paper, put it back in the tin with the stone on top, put the lid on and replaced the two elastic bands. Hawke held out his hand and Sebastian gave him the tin, he went onto the balcony and launched it into the garden next door. There was a satisfying plop as the tin landed in the Pool of Petrification.

'Challenge accepted,' shouted Hawke.

He would like to have seen the twins trying to fish the tin out of the pool but he didn't want them the think he'd deliberately aimed for the water. He went back into the Command Bunker to work out how they were going to tackle the Assault course in the morning.

11

The Challenge

'Come on, come on, we don't want to be late,' Hawke grumbled.

'I've got five more minutes piano practice to do before we can go, so don't keep interrupting me.'

Hawke slouched out of the living room and left Sebastian to finish his practice. He sat on the bottom of the stairs and tried not to watch the clock as the minutes ticked their way towards 10 o' clock. He knew Sebastian wouldn't cut his practice short, even though no one was watching him or making him do it; he just loved playing the piano.

The doorbell went. Hawke opened the door to Spike.

'I didn't know if you'd be round next-door already.'

'No,' sighed Hawke, 'we can't go until Sebastian's finished.'

'Hello Stephen,' said Hawke's Mum as she passed him in the hallway, 'are you going round to play at the twin's house too?'

'We're not going to play,' began Spike, 'we're going….

'We're going to help them in the garden,' interrupted Hawke before Spike revealed their true reason for visiting Tom and Sam.

'That's really kind of you both, I was wondering why you'd got your old tracksuits on.'

'I'm ready now,' announced Sebastian.

'Ready for what?' asked Mum.

'To go round next door.'

'Oh no you're not, I'm not having you using

spades and forks and risk injuring your hands, you've got a concert in two days at the Village Hall. How are you going to play if you've got blisters or a broken arm?'

Hawke thought his Mum had a point. If she knew the truth about *The Challenge* she would have banned them both from going, in case either of them got hurt. Hawke thought he ought to say something before Sebastian spoilt it for the rest of them.

'Can't Sebastian come with us and just watch?'

'Well as long as he doesn't do anything to injure himself and I shall expect you to make sure he comes home in one piece.'

'He'll be fine Mum, promise.'

When they were all out of the house Sebastian turned on Hawke.

'Why did you lie to Mum?'

'She wouldn't have let either of us go if she'd known we'd been challenged to walk a plank over the Pool of Petrification.'

Spike looked puzzled.

'I thought you said it was only pretend?'

'The petrification bit is but the plank and the pool will be real enough, that's why I told you to put your old track suit on; the gardening was an excuse in case we get dirty.'

'That's brilliant Hawke, I'd never have thought of that.'

'But it still means I won't be able to join in,' Sebastian pointed out.

'You can if you're the judge and record keeper. Tom and Sam know you don't cheat and someone has to record all the times; how else will we know who's won? You can use this.' Hawke pulled out a stopwatch from his pocket and dangled it in front of Sebastian's nose.

Hawke pulled out a stopwatch from his pocket.

'I also got you these,' said Hawke as he pulled a pad and pen out of the other pocket, 'just in case they're not prepared; it will show them we mean business.'

'Alright,' agreed Sebastian, 'I don't mind being the timekeeper, but only if Tom and Sam agree.'

They went to the front door and rang the bell; they didn't want Tom and Sam to know they could get into their garden through the two loose planks in the fence. Hawke wondered if the twin's parents knew about the assault course. After ringing the bell again, Sam opened the door.

'We got your soggy reply and presumed you'd accepted, it was all smudged by the time we'd fished it out of the pool, the tin wasn't waterproof.'

Tom appeared behind Sam and opened the door wider.

'Come on through, we've been planning this for ages but we needed some rain to make the slime pit sludgy.'

'It still wasn't muddy enough so we've watered it again this morning,' explained Sam, 'so if you fall off when you're trying to swing over it you'll be slimed up good and proper.'

'How've you planned to work out who wins?' asked Hawke.

'Wins?' the twin's said together.

'If it's a challenge and we've accepted, there has to be a winner,' explained Hawke.

'We just thought you'd like a bit of fun,' replied Tom, 'Dad said we could do it before he sorts the garden out.'

Hawke smiled and winked at Sebastian.

'Well it's a good thing we brought a timekeeper along.'

'I'm very trustworthy,' said Sebastian, 'I can time everyone as they go round and then we can see who's got the fastest time, if that's ok with you?'

'Great!' exclaimed Tom, 'but don't you want to have a turn too?'

'I'm not allowed.'

Sam put her hand on Sebastian's shoulder and gave him her best smile.

'You'll be a brilliant timekeeper.'

'What's the prize for the winner?' asked Spike.

'Prize?' said the twins together.

'If there's going to be a winner you need to have a prize,' explained Hawke.

'We've got this,' said Tom as he pulled Hawke's torch out from his back pocket, 'this can be the prize.'

Hawke could see Sebastian was about to announce they had one just like that at home so before he could begin his sentence Hawke elbowed him in the back.

'It must be 10 o'clock by now, shall we make a start?'

Tom and Sam led the way into the back garden. Hawke noticed a large ground sheet had been spread over the patch where he'd tripped over the roots. A plank had been laid across the swimming pool; it wasn't narrow so crossing it was going to be easy. On one of the patio slabs the word *START* had been chalked and a box drawn around it.

'How do you want to choose who goes first?' asked Sam.

'Size,' suggested Spike.

'That's only because you're the biggest,' complained Hawke.

'It doesn't have to be the biggest first, it could be the smallest,' suggested Sebastian.

'That's fine with me,' replied Sam.

'And me,' agreed Hawke.

'Yep, no problem with that,' said Tom, 'so it'll be Sam, Valentine, me, then Spike.'

'Can we get one thing straight,' snapped Hawke, 'no one calls me Valentine, it's Hawke, OK!'

'OK,' the twins agreed, but Sam had a little giggle to herself, which bothered Hawke a bit.

Spike looked puzzled.

'Why am I last?'

'Because you're the tallest,' explained Sebastian.

Tom coughed to gain everyone's attention.

'Let the Challenge begin,' he announced loudly.

'But we don't know what we've got to do,' said Spike.

'It's not going to be fair,' grumbled Hawke, 'I bet you've both had lots of practice.'

'Neither of us have been round the course,' Sam replied, 'but we can show you the route.'

Sam explained what they had to do for each part of the challenge. Next to the starting line on the patio several cones had been placed in a wavy line; they went in and out of some overgrown bushes.

'This is the Scented Slalom,' she began.

'Why's it scented?' asked Spike.

'Well if you bump into any of the bushes you'll

get lavender all over you and it really pongs,' laughed Tom as he held his nose with his fingers to make the point.

'OK, I've got that,' said Hawke, 'we weave in and out without touching the bushes.'

'On the skateboard!' announced Sam.

'Oh!' said Hawke and Spike together; neither of them had ever used a skateboard before.

'What's next?' asked Spike looking at a series of planks, which had been raised off the ground, each on a stack of four bricks.

'That was my idea,' said Sam proudly, 'they're The Gateways of Doom!'

'She likes playing gymkhana,' explained Tom, 'so she uses these as horse jumps on her pretend pony!'

'But not today,' continued Sam.

'That should be easy,' laughed Spike 'I play gymkhana with my cousin Sarah and her jumps are a lot higher.'

'You have to go over the first one then under the second and keep doing it until you get to the end,' explained Sam, 'it should be quite a challenge; especially if we're doing it against the clock!'

'Where's the tomb?' asked Spike as he looked around the garden.

'Under the groundsheet,' replied Tom as he pointed to the bottom of the garden, 'you have to find a bone in there; Dad put them in so we don't know where they are; there's five altogether.'

'See,' Spike whispered in Hawke's ear, 'it's got to be a real tomb if there's bones in there.'

'The Slime Pit is easy,' continued Tom, 'you have to swing over it on the rope.

Hawke, Spike and Sebastian looked dismally at the area of thick, oozing mud, which was underneath the spreading branches of a large tree. A thick rope had been tied onto its lowest branch.

Hawke nodded towards the swimming pool.

'I presume that's the Pool of Petrification

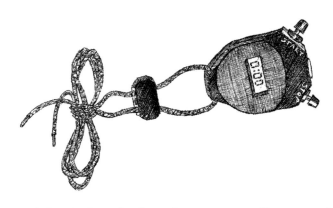

and that's the plank we've got to walk across.'

'It is,' agreed Tom.

'Well that's the course,' said Sam proudly, 'are you ready to begin?'

'We are,' the boys replied together.

'One question,' began Sebastian, 'when do you want me to stop the watch?'

'How about when we get back to the urn,' suggested Tom as he pointed to a large empty flowerpot in the middle of the patio, 'we can put the bones we find in it.'

'Sounds ok to me,' announced Sebastian. Everyone nodded in agreement.

12

The Assault Course

'Three, two, one, go!' shouted Sebastian as he gave Sam the countdown to begin her challenge.

Hawke watched as Sam bashed her way through the bushes. She didn't seem to mind the overpowering smell of lavender. It was a good tactic and gained her a lot of time.

'Wow!' exclaimed Spike as Sam ran towards the Gateways of Doom.

She jumped over and crawled under each of the obstacles with the greatest of ease.

Everyone watched Sam's progress around the course.

'Come on Sam,' shouted Tom encouragingly.

Sam lifted up the groundsheet and wriggled underneath. She seemed to be in the Tomb of Misfortune for ages; when she finally emerged at the other end she was triumphantly holding a bone.

'It's a dog biscuit!' exclaimed Spike with obvious disappointment.

'It wouldn't be hygienic to use real bones,' Sebastian informed him.

Before Spike could reply Tom started jumping up and down and shouting loudly at his sister.

'Come on Sam, come on, grab the rope.'

Sam leant over and pulled the swing towards her, she nimbly leapt on and started to rock to and fro. Hawke watched intently to see how she was going to get off without sliding into the Slime Pit. Sam launched herself off sideways and went straight into a judo roll; she easily cleared the oozing mud. In a flash she was up the steps on the side of the swimming pool and almost ran across the plank; she never once looked down into the Pool of Petrification. She raced up to the patio and dropped her bone into the urn. Sebastian stopped the clock and wrote Sam's time down on the pad.

'A brilliant time,' he told her.

'How brilliant?' enquired Hawke.

'You'll have to wait until everyone's been round to find out.'

It was Hawke's turn next. He steadied himself on the skateboard ready to begin as Sebastian counted down. He wobbled badly as he tried to get around the cones without touching the bushes. The smell was awful as he brushed his knee against the last bush. He wove his way in and out of the Gateways of Doom very quickly and even got a clap from Sam. He knew there'd be roots underneath the groundsheet as he entered The Tomb of Misfortune, only this time he wouldn't trip up because he was already on the ground. He was lucky and found a bone straight away. As he burst out from under the cover he could hear everyone shouting his name.

The swing wasn't as easy as Sam had made it look. Hawke managed to get on but getting off was more difficult. He knew if he tried to roll like Sam he'd probably break his shoulder. He swung backwards and forwards trying to decide how best to avoid the mud. Everyone shouted and cheered him on. He knew the seconds were ticking by, he had to jump, he got ready to launch himself but his hand was so sweaty he lost his grip and slid. He landed half in and half out of the mud.

Hawke wiped his gunged up hand on his tracksuit and set off at a run. The last part was easy; he might not be a judo expert or a musician but he was fairly good at gymnastics. He quickly crossed the Pool of Petrification. There was a great cheer as he dropped his bone into the urn.

'Another brilliant time,' announced Sebastian.

Tom went next. Hawke watched as he made

his way to the Tomb of Misfortune without a problem. If Tom kept this up he'd easily beat Hawke's time, but instead of coming straight out, he didn't appear. Sam looked worried and started shouting for Tom to hurry; it seemed to take ages before his head finally appeared. Everyone cheered, and Hawke realised he was cheering too. Tom got on and off the swing easily, which impressed Hawke. This gained him some time but he was unable to run across the plank. Hawke thought Tom looked frightened as he made his way carefully to the other side. His bone eventually landed in the urn.

'Well done Tom,' said Sebastian.

'I know it wasn't a brilliant time,' replied Tom, 'but it was still fun.'

'You were great on the swing,' said Hawke knowing how much of a problem it had been for him.

'Come on Spike,' said Sam, 'your turn.'

Spike must have hit every bush with a different part of his body as he made his way through the Slalom.

Spike must have hit every bush with a different part of his body as he made his way through the Slalom; the overpowering smell of lavender made him sneeze. By the time he'd cleared the Gateways of Doom he'd bumped his head twice. Hawke shouted encouragement to him as he entered the Tomb of Misfortune. Within seconds he'd found not one, but two bones. He'd made up a lot of lost time when he reached the swing. Hawke held his breath but Spike cleared the mud and did a spectacular judo roll onto the grass at the other side. Unfortunately it wasn't quite as good as Sam's; Spike was unable to get up quickly enough and the momentum of his roll sent him sliding backwards into the mud. He was plastered from head to foot. He was still clutching both the bones and had to put them in his mouth so he could climb up the steps on the side of the pool. Again Hawke held his breath as he watched Spike climb up onto the plank. He'd only taken one step when his muddy feet began to slither and slide around. He flapped his arms wildly trying to regain his balance but it was no use. He toppled off and hit the water with a resounding smack.

'Oh no!' wailed Tom, 'Dad'll kill us; we're not supposed to get the pool dirty.

When Spike emerged out of the pool he still had the two bones between his teeth. Luckily all the mud had been washed off his clothes.

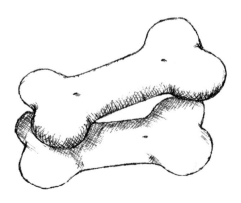

He clambered out, dripped his way to the urn and dropped one of the bones inside. He kept the other one and took a bite out of it.

'Ugh!' everyone cried.

'They're not that bad you know,' Spike informed them, 'these are better than my Nan gets for her dog.'

They all pulled a face as Spike chomped his way through the dog biscuit.

Sebastian wrote down Spike's time.

'Would you like to know who's won?' he asked.

Tom and Sam were really worried about the swirling mud in the swimming pool. They knew they were going to be in trouble.

'In fourth place,' announced Sebastian, 'Spike, with one minute and forty seconds.'

There was a great cheer from Hawke.

'In third place, Tom, with one minute and twenty five seconds.'

Sam joined in with the cheer and Spike shook

Tom's hand.

'In second place, Sam,' said Sebastian, 'with one minute and twelve seconds.'

Everyone cheered again and Tom gave his sister a hug.

'The winner with one minute and ten seconds is Hawke,' Sebastian announced with a big smile on his face.

'You win the torch then,' said Tom as he reluctantly went to collect if from the windowsill.

'I'm sorry about your pool,' said Spike.

'So are we!' exclaimed Sam.

'I think we're going to be in big trouble,' replied Tom, 'but Dad did say we could have an assault course.'

'Would it help if I went and told him it was an accident and it was my fault, I'd say I was very sorry?' asked Spike.

'Not really,' replied Tom, 'but thanks for offering.'

'We ought to go,' said Sebastian, 'thanks for a great time.'

'Yes, thanks,' said Hawke.

When they were back in the Command Bunker, reliving the events of the morning, Hawke realized they'd managed, at last, to put the twins pool out of action. Somehow it didn't feel as good as he'd thought it would. They'd be in trouble and he knew how that felt, it had happened to him often enough.

'I like the twins,' said Sebastian.

'So do I,' replied Spike.

Hawke grunted.

'Perhaps we ought to ask them if they'd like to join Hawke & Co,' said Spike, 'it might make up for us getting all that mud in their pool.'

'They'd have somewhere to play for the rest of the summer if they said yes, and I'm sure we could have lots of fun together in the Bunker,' replied Sebastian.

'We'll go and see them in the morning,' agreed Hawke, 'they can join us, but only if I get my apology.'

'I'm sure Tom's sorry he called you an oik,' said Sebastian, 'you'll see, he'll apologise straight away.'

Hawke grunted again.

'I ought to go home and change now,' said Spike, 'see you tomorrow.'

That night when Hawke and Sebastian lay in bed, Hawke pulled out his torch. He was glad he'd got it back. He switched it on and started to make patterns on the wall. He'd only got as far as the window when the light dimmed and went out.

'Oh brilliant,' he grumbled.

'Flat batteries,' Sebastian informed him.

'I know, go to sleep, no one asked for your opinion little brother.'

ACKNOWLEDGEMENTS

I'd like to thank Ron
for his honesty and constancy,

Natalie for her artistic skills,

Dad, Molly and Geoffrey
for their help and encouragement,

Yvonne and Aidan
for their attention to detail
and support,

Callum and Shreya,
who read and commented
on the first draft

and
everyone who's shared this journey.

An interview with...

Valentine Sibelius Hawke

What's your favourite sport?
Football

What's your favourite food?
Burgers and Chips but we don't have it at
home because Mum's a vegetarian.

Is there anything you don't like?
My name... perfume and girls

Who's your best friend?
Spike

Do you have a pet?
No

If you could have a pet what would it be?
A dog.

Where is your favourite place?
The seaside

Do you have a hobby?
No I'm not very good at making things.

An interview with...

SEBASTIAN

Sebastian Amadeus Hawke

What's your favourite sport?
I'm not allowed to play sports.

What's your favourite food?
Fish fingers and baked beans with lots
of tomato ketchup.

Is there anything you don't like?
I don't like it when my big brother thinks
he's always right because he isn't.

Who's your best friend?
I'm friends with everyone.

Do you have a pet?
No

If you could have a pet what would it be?
A goldfish and I'd call it Beethoven.

Where is your favourite place?
The library.

Do you have a hobby?
I play the piano, violin and I sing.
I like performing. An interview with...

An interview with...

SPIKE

Stephen Pike

What's your favourite sport?
Football.

What's your favourite food?
Pizza and chips with lots of
different toppings and a milk shake.

Is there anything you don't like?
I don't like having to go to Judo class
because I'm not very good at it.

Who's your best friend?
Hawke.

Do you have a pet?
No but we sometimes look after Nan's dog.

If you could have a pet what would it be?
A snake, I like Corn Snakes best.

Where is your favourite place?
Adventure Parks.

Do you have a hobby?
I like making things, anything,
especially models.

Some of your comments...

I enjoyed the book a lot.

SHREYA

So did I

fun to share

I ♡ Hawke

he he he

Getting wet wasn't funny.

It was funny.

CALLUM

ha ha ha

I liked reading about boys getting into trouble.

SARAH

a great bedtime story

z z z z z

A marvellous read for boys and girls alike, unputdownable. Leaves you wanting more, can't wait for the next episode.

AIDAN

...if you'd like to comment too please email

pengridionbooks@btinternet.com

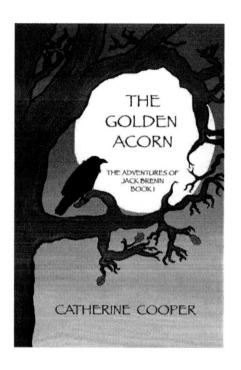

Jack Brenin's life changes the moment he finds a golden acorn lying in the grass. He gets caught up in an extraordinary magical adventure and enters a world he only believed existed in legend. He's sure he's been mistaken for someone else. He's neither brave nor strong so how could he possibly be 'The One' an ancient prophecy speaks about? He's no idea why he's expected to help, unsure if he wants to, or even if he can.

…the whole book has a dreamlike quality, which should appeal to the child in all of us.

Reviewer – Sally Bunn   Rating – ★★★★★

COMING SOON

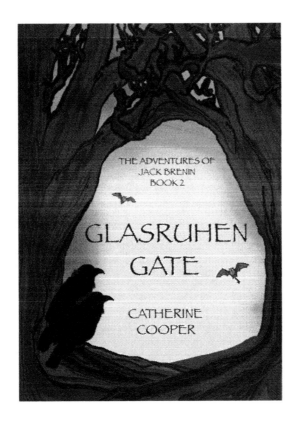

The magic and adventure continue in
Glasruhen Gate